Other Books by this Author:

Out of the Storm

The Bridge Club Series

Deception Bridge
Broken Contracts
Premonition Bridge

The Whispering Art Series

Watercolor Whispers
Whispered Warnings
Waiting for the Whisper

Christmas Melody

GLORIA BOSTIC

Year of the Book
135 Glen Avenue
Glen Rock, PA 17327

Print ISBN: 978-1-64649-287-9
eBook ISBN: 978-1-64649-288-6

Dedication

This book is dedicated to my family
for all the joy I feel as they
surround me each Christmas day.

1 Winter Sky

November 2016

Death alters life. Melody stared out at the horizon and pulled her balaclava up to ward off the sting of salt and sand. Unlike the warm ocean breeze of summer, this icy wind pricked every inch of exposed skin on her body... but it couldn't compare to the pain of loss she still bore... especially as the holidays drew near.

Melody's thoughts went back to the last time the Patterson family had huddled together searching the sky, ignoring the cold until they found the vision they sought. It was nearly two years ago now, but the memory was as vivid as though it was yesterday.

"There!" Melody had exclaimed. "There it is!" And, like every Christmas Eve as far back as she could remember, they had stared in wonder at the bright shining star in the east which they believed led the magi to the manger long, long ago.

Then they'd dashed back inside to warm themselves by the fire.

Melody recalled how she and her older sister, Chelsea, cradled warm cups of hot chocolate, settled in with their mom, and waited for their father to begin.

"For unto you is born this day in the city of David a savior, which is Christ the Lord. And this shall be a sign unto you..." Ken Patterson had read from his well-worn Bible, as he had every Christmas Eve as far back as Melody could remember.

The next morning, Melody had awoken to her sister's whispered words. *"Mel, did you hear that?"*

"What?" She rubbed her eyes and listened. "What is that? It, it sounds like yipping."

"I know, right? Do you think—"

Before Chelsea could finish the sentence, Melody had jumped out of bed, grabbed her robe, and headed for the door. *"Oh my gosh! They finally got us a dog, Chels!"*

The two girls had sprinted down the stairs, and there, next to the big Christmas tree in the bay window of the living room, they spied a crate with the cutest puppy Melody had ever seen. The adorable ball of fur leapt about, pawed at the cage, and yipped with joy at their arrival.

Melody had been the first to reach the crate, and within seconds she was cradling the sheltie puppy in her arms while it happily licked her face. It was sable with a white collar and a tiny white marking on its face.

"Look Chels, it looks like a star! Oh, let's name her Star! It's Christmas... so it's perfect, don't you think?"

"Sounds perfect to me." Their father's voice had startled them both and sent them rushing into their parents' arms with hugs of gratitude.

Melody choked back tears at the memory of her father's rich baritone voice. A voice she would never hear again. It was hard to breathe.

Death is a thief.

"Star, come!" In an instant her constant companion was by her side, no longer that tiny puppy. Melody stooped down and rubbed behind the dog's perfectly tipped ears, gazed into her bright cheerful expression, then buried her face in the soft white mane.

"And the next morning, there you were," she whispered to Star who licked her face in response. When Melody tried to stand back up, Star—still a puppy at heart—jumped up, knocked Melody off balance, and smothered her with kisses until they were rolling around on the cold sand.

"You silly girl!" Melody laughed as she struggled to get to her feet. "You always make me feel better, but it's freezing. C'mon." Melody stuffed her hands in her pockets and turned back toward the house—with Star at her heels—knowing she would never again see her father in that chair or hear his rich baritone read those words. Death had taken that all away.

Star was the last Christmas gift she would ever receive from her father. Maybe that's what made Star so special.

***

December 24, 2014

"It's beautiful, girls." Ken Patterson grabbed his camera. "Let's get a picture of the two of you sitting in front of the tree." This had become the new tradition when Melody turned eleven and Chelsea thirteen and their parents were certain both girls were wise to who decorated the tree after they went to bed. Ken had to admit it was nice not to have to stay up all night making the magic happen.

After taking several pictures of his daughters, Ken turned the camera over to Chelsea so she could get a couple of shots of him and their mom, Judy. Then the four of them were off to church for the Christmas Eve candlelight service.

They had to arrive earlier than most so Melody and her dad could get to the choir room, then don their red and white robes and get ready for the procession. This was the most beautiful service of the year, and the church Melody loved was adorned with red bows at the end of each pew, luscious poinsettias everywhere, and the "candles" in the darkness. It was magical. The glorious celebration of Christ's birth ended with the triumphant singing of the Hallelujah Chorus from Handel's *Messiah*.

Melody had been blessed with a special voice and had no difficulty executing the quick, complex passages of the music. With her gift and ability to sing soprano or alto, the choir director, Mr. Sipe, had been excited to have her join even though at thirteen, she was much younger than the other members. Eighteen-year-old Carol Blair—the closest to her age—was a strong soprano, so Mr. Sipe had gladly added young Melody to the alto section. Thrilled to join the chorus of voices each Sunday morning, she knew someday she'd be reaching the high notes of the melody—maybe even on Broadway.

Everyone seemed amazed by Melody's range and the power of her voice for one so young, but Melody knew where she got her talent. It was from the baritone standing one step up behind her in the choir loft, her dad.

Ken's rich baritone rang out, "Forever and ever, Hallelujah, Hallelujah!"

Melody and the other three altos followed, then the four sopranos' voices sang…"King of Kings, and Lord of Lords"

As the chorus built to the awesome crescendo, Melody saw her mother and sister standing in the third pew singing with all the joy of their Savior's birth. She saw the elation on their faces and those of the other congregants. This moment was so glorious, it would be emblazoned in Melody's mind for the rest of her life… especially since it would never—could never—be duplicated.

After the service, although it was late, they hurried home, bundled up, and went out on the beach to find the star. Melody spotted it immediately, and the rest of the family looked in the direction she pointed. After a moment of standing in awe, her father said, "Now I think we'd better go in and get warm."

Once inside, Ken Patterson stoked the fire while Judy went to the kitchen and soon returned with a tray filled with steaming mugs of cocoa. Then, and this was something Melody would never forget, their father sat in his big leather chair, while she and her sister sat on the couch with their mother sipping hot chocolate and listening to him read the familiar words. They could have recited it with him by then, yet they loved to hear him read the story of the true meaning of Christmas. The moment was like a familiar warm embrace.

"And the shepherds returned, glorifying and praising God for all the things they had heard and seen, as it was told unto them." Ken Patterson closed the family Bible and beamed. "Amen, and off to bed with you!"

Although the memories were fading, when Melody closed her eyes, she could still see his smile and his eyes filled with love.

***

The following Christmas Eve, no one could bear the thought of reading the story. They went through the motions of celebrating the holiday—even put the usual trimmings on the tree—but it was missing the joy. Fifteen-year-old Melody found no pleasure in singing the Hallelujah Chorus at the Christmas Eve church service. She no longer sang with the choir. She was too angry with God for taking her father away. No matter how much their mother tried to make things feel normal, the spirit of Christmas was gone from the Patterson household and from Melody's heart.

The day after Thanksgiving, 2015

Melody was glad to have Thanksgiving over and done with. She could think of nothing to be thankful for this year, and worse yet, now everyone was getting excited about Christmas. Every store was bedecked with trees and lights while Christmas music played to get the "Black Friday" shoppers in the mood.

However, the members of the Patterson household didn't even want to think about the upcoming holiday. They had said their final farewells to Ken Patterson a mere two months earlier. Melody still couldn't believe he was gone. One day he came home from work, had dinner, and spent time with his family. The next day, he went to work and never came home.

They said it was a massive heart attack. Melody was inconsolable. While Chelsea grieved with and tried to help her mother, Melody withdrew, sharing her grief with no one but Star. After the funeral, she retreated into her room, coming out only at her sister's urging.

"Melody, please. Mom is having such a hard time right now, and she's worried about you. That doesn't help." Her sister's words filled Melody with conflicting emotions. She didn't want to hurt her mother, but neither did she want to sit at the table—the table with an empty chair where her father should be sitting.

"I can't, Chels. I just can't sit out there." Melody buried her head in her pillow and threw her arm over Star who nuzzled concern for her favorite person.

She was relieved when her sister quietly left the room, but moments later there was a gentle knock on the door and her mother's voice broke when she spoke.

"I brought you a plate, Mel. I understand what you're feeling, but could you please try to eat something?" Judy Patterson placed the plate and utensils on the desk and turned to leave.

"Mom... thank you." She wanted to hug her mother and tell her it would be okay, but she couldn't bring herself to utter words she didn't believe. How could it ever be okay?

Melody ate the food without tasting it, then left her room to help clean up the kitchen. That was the beginning of her days of going through the motions.

She returned to school the next week, saw her friends, accepted their condolences, and did the work required, all while feeling nothing.

When the numbness finally subsided, anger took its place. Melody's anger was scattered everywhere and directed at everything and everyone for months. Even her best friend, Denise Henley, had been the recipient of one of her outbursts, and it might have ended their friendship of many years if Denise hadn't been tolerant and accepted her apology.

It was Chelsea who finally broke through the anger with words that pierced her sister's heart one Sunday afternoon when the three of them returned home from church.

"I miss seeing you in the choir loft." Her mom was hanging her coat in the closet when she said it.

Melody lashed out at her. "What about Dad? Don't you miss seeing him up there?" As soon as the words had fallen from her lips, she wanted to scoop them back up.

Her guilt doubled when her sister pulled her into the kitchen. "What's wrong with you?" It was a shouted whisper, and the anger on Chelsea's face was not typical of the easy-going older Patterson girl. "You're not the only one who misses him, you know!" The words poured out like they had broken through a dam. "Mom lost her husband! We can't even imagine what she's going through... and you're not the only one who lost their dad!" Chelsea stormed out of the room leaving Melody feeling lower than a snake slithering under the leaves.

Embarrassed and ashamed, she slithered into the living room where she found Chelsea and their mom in a tearful embrace. Through all the guilt and regret, she could only utter two words. "I'm sorry," she whispered, and seconds later Ken Patterson's three girls held fast in a healing embrace.

Leaning on each other for support, none of them knew how much their lives would change.

2 Pushing On

Christmas 2015

The Pattersons went through the motions that Christmas, decorating the tree at Judy's urging. She told them it would help her, but in truth she hoped it would help them, too.

Judy could not imagine Christmas without her husband. She and Ken had married twenty years earlier, right after college, but they had known each other since elementary school. A life without her husband was incomprehensible, and yet this was the life she had been given... and she had to live it for her girls.

Oh Kenny, why?

She missed him every moment of every day. The brave face she forced herself to wear for her daughters' sake crumbled as she laid her head on her pillow each night. Tonight would be no different, but it wasn't time for tears... not yet.

She watched as her girls put the last of the Christmas balls on the tree. They had decided to forego hanging the shiny, silver icicles this year. When they were finished, she removed the bubble wrap from four new ornaments and placed them on the tree herself. "I ordered these a while ago. I didn't know then how difficult it would be to hang them."

They laughed when they saw the first few ornaments. On the first, Chelsea held two devil fingers behind her little sister's head, and in the second one, they were making silly faces with crossed eyes and tongues sticking out. The third showed two innocent looking young ladies, hands folded before them like angels. That one brought the most laughter as they all proclaimed it propaganda. But it was the final ornament that cut the laughter short.

Chelsea gasped and Melody's chin quivered as they gazed at the happy and smiling Judy and Ken. "He's still with us, you know," Judy said. Her voice cracked, but she believed it was true. She knew her husband somehow was with them… and yet he wasn't.

Wiping away the tears and grabbing their coats, the somber trio headed to church, but instead of the usual two, all three Pattersons stood in that third pew as the choir led the congregation in the Hallelujah Chorus. To Judy's ear it sounded somewhat hollow without her husband's rich baritone. She assumed no one else noticed the difference until she glanced over at her youngest daughter and saw the tears sliding down her cheeks. That's when she realized Melody was mouthing the words without making a sound. The music was missing from her Melody.

No one spoke on the ride home. There was nothing to say. Judy wondered what to do when they got there. Should she offer to read the Christmas story the way Ken had done every Christmas Eve since the girls were two and four years old? If she tried, could she even get through it?

"Good night, Mom." Melody kissed her on the cheek and, followed by Star, headed to her room without even taking off her coat.

"Good night, Mel. Sleep tight." The phrase came out of habit, but she doubted she or anyone else in the house would actually sleep *tight* that night. Haunting memories of Christmas past danced in their heads… and the loss was too great. But at least the decision about reading the familiar Bible story was taken out of her hands. She looked at her other daughter standing alone and looking so forlorn. "Are you all right, sweetie?"

"Yeah, I guess. How about you, Mom? Are you okay?"

"Of course." It was a lie, and they both knew it, but what good would it do to say otherwise? "Do you want some hot cider before bed?"

"No, I think I'm going to turn in too." Chelsea turned to leave then hesitated and turned back. "Tomorrow's gonna be hard, Mom, but we'll get through it."

She hugged her, and Judy held on a little longer than normal before replying, "Yes. We're going to be okay." But she wasn't sure she believed that lie either.

3 Volleyball

Life did go on for Judy, Chelsea, and Melody, but it was a new life, a different life, a life with a missing piece. They had opened presents that Christmas morning, hugged, and thanked each other for their thoughtful gifts, and sat down to their traditional ham dinner, but the typical merriment was missing.

Melody wondered how she could even keep going. Yet as one day followed another, she kept to her usual routine. Life moved on.

The long, cold, lonely winter melted into spring, but the joyous feeling of the season did not lighten her mood. Even when school ended for the year and there was time for summer fun, Melody walked on the beach just steps from her home—a beachcomber searching for something beyond her reach—but had no desire to dive into the rolling waves, play volleyball in the sand, or swim laps in their pool.

She usually took Star out on the beach where they played early in the morning, but it didn't seem fitting to have fun even then. Judy had urged her to talk to a professional—someone to help her through the grieving process—but Melody wouldn't take her mother's advice. She couldn't see the point of talking to some stranger about her sadness. It was hers and hers alone to hold.

Whenever she caught herself laughing or having fun with friends, she scolded herself. Until she met Zach.

It was June fifteenth—Melody would never forget it—that she saw him for the first time. After taking her usual morning walk near the water's edge, she spread out her towel and sat on the beach to rest and watch a group of kids about her age playing a vigorous game of beach volleyball. She recognized many of them from school, but there was one stranger who caught her eye. His hair was the color of the sand beneath his feet, and when, without warning, he approached her, she saw his eyes were the color of the sea. Unlike the sad blue-gray eyes reflected in her mirror, his ocean blue eyes danced like the waves breaking on the shore.

"Hey, can you help us out? Anne Marie said she's gotta quit." The stranger pointed to a fragile-looking young girl limping away from the group. "She twisted her ankle."

"Oh, I, I'm not very good—"

The good-looking stranger literally grabbed her by the hand and dragged her into the game. "Don't worry about it. You're really helping us out. I'm Zach, by the way."

"I'm Melody," she answered feeling more shy than normal.

"This is Melody, everybody. She's gonna fill in for Anne Marie."

Melody waved and forced a smile in response to the greetings from the group. She hadn't played in quite a while, but there wasn't time to worry about that as Zach served the next volley and the game resumed. She relaxed a little seeing that these weren't a bunch of Olympic level players, and before long she was totally focused on the ball.

At the end of the game, when she was catching her breath and brushing off the sand, Zach approached again. "Thanks for helping us out... it's Melody, right?" Melody nodded. "And I forgive you for lying."

"What? What are you talking about?" Confused and a bit indignant, Melody looked up into blue-green eyes filled with merriment.

"You said you weren't very good, but it looks like you're better than most of us. I think you've had a lot of practice. So, are you a local or just vacationing here?"

"Local." Melody pointed in the direction of her house. "What about you?"

"We're local as of a few weeks ago. My folks bought a place between here and the boardwalk. I'm told it used to be the Talbot's place, but now it's the Farley's. I mean that's our last name—

Farley." Zach's big smile warmed Melody more than the sun. "So maybe we'll be seeing a lot of each other, huh?"

"I don't know... maybe." Melody picked up her towel and shook out the sand. "I've gotta get home. See ya."

She turned and jogged across the beach without waiting for a response, but she smiled as she heard him call after her, "Hope so!"

Back at the house, Melody found her mother sitting on the screened porch with a book and her usual morning glass of water with lemon. "You were gone longer than usual." Judy closed her book. "Did you walk farther this morning, or were you just soaking in the sun?"

"Actually, I was playing volleyball."

Melody saw the surprise flash across her mother's face before she replaced it with a big grin. "That's great! Did you have fun?"

Melody shrugged. "It was all right." Before her mother could pursue the conversation further, Melody hurried inside and greeted Star who wagged with joy and followed her to her room.

Melody breezed by her sister's doorway in no mood to chat, closed her own door, and plopped down on the bed. She laughed at Star's happy kisses, then got up and moved into the sunlight. She had a view of the beach from her bedroom window, but her gaze went far beyond the sand as she stared out at the waves rolling in. Looking beyond the sea to the horizon, she saw the one beautiful puffy cloud. The sun's rays shone down from it like a path to the sea. *Oh, Daddy...*

Melody imagined her father sitting on that cloud looking down on her. *I'm sorry.* She wondered how she could begin to have fun—to be happy—when he wasn't there. But it *had* been fun, and she couldn't help wanting to see sandy-haired Zach again.

Then as her gaze returned to the shoreline, she noticed a couple walking down the beach. Though they weren't close enough for her to be certain, the guy had familiar blond hair, and wasn't that the color he was wearing?

"Hey, what's going on, Mel?" Melody swung around to see her sister standing in the doorway with a look of concern on her face. "Are you okay?" Chelsea stooped down to pet Star who had hopped off the bed to greet her.

"Yeah, just... I don't know. Tired, I guess."

"Okay, listen. You've gotta snap out of this. Ever since Dad died, you've been walking around like you're half dead too. C'mon."

Melody felt her face crumbling. She didn't want to cry again. It seemed like she'd cried enough for a lifetime.

She took a deep breath, blew it out slowly, and looked up at Chelsea. "You know what? You're right." It was like a dislocated shoulder popped back into place. Melody made a silent decision to stop dwelling on missing her dad. "And I actually kind of met someone this morning."

"What? Who?"

"Some guy—his name's Zach." She sat on the edge of her bed and grinned up at Chelsea. "And he's gorgeous!" Both girls giggled and flopped on the bed.

Chelsea pulled one leg under her. "Okay, that's more like it. Give... tell me more."

That was a turning point for Melody. She told her sister all about the volleyball game and the boy who had dragged her into it. She even admitted to her sister and to herself that she'd had fun.

For just a little while, she had forgotten to be sad.

4 Around the Fire

"Hey, there you are!" Denise ran to meet Melody. "I'm glad you decided to come."

Since her father's death, Melody hadn't spent as much time with her best friend as she used to. They had still seen each other at school every day and texted a lot, but she hadn't joined Denise for shopping, hanging out, or doing anything with their theater group. Even her voice lessons had been a chore. But Melody was ready for all that to change, and she was looking forward to the bonfire on the beach.

"Who all's coming tonight?" Melody asked as they tread through the sand. She kind of hoped there might be a new boy there.

"Most everybody that's usually here. And, oh yeah, there's this new guy, and he's so cute!" Melody's spirits lifted thinking she must be talking about Zach. "I think I'm in love." Denise laughed when she said it, but Melody suddenly saw red flags flying.

Melody laughed with her friend hoping they weren't going gaga over the same boy. "You're in love with every good-looking guy you see, Dee," she teased.

"Haha, whatever. But seriously girl, wait 'til you see him."

I bet I already have. Melody kept her groan inside.

A half dozen kids were already sitting around the fire, and a burst of laughter erupted as the girls approached.

"Hey, it's Denise and Melody," someone called out as they widened their circle to let them in. Melody greeted everyone as she scanned the group looking for one face, but it wasn't there.

"Darn, he's not here." Denise had been doing the same search. "Wait. I think that's him." She nodded her head to the south, and

Melody saw two figures walking up the beach toward them. "Oh crap... he's with somebody."

Melody squinted in the waning light of dusk, but the moonlight was enough for her to see it was Zach, and he was not alone. Walking by his side was Anne Marie, the striking brunette who'd limped away from the volleyball game.

Again, the circle widened, making room for the newcomers. "How's it going?" someone asked amongst the many greetings.

"See what I mean?" Denise whispered.

"What?"

"About how cute he is... don't you think so?"

"Yeah, I guess." In truth, Melody wasn't guessing. She wholeheartedly agreed. "But it looks like you're out of luck. He's already got a girlfriend."

"Yeah. I'm pretty sure I hate her."

Melody looked across the bonfire and realized Zach was staring at her with a quizzical smile. Then realization lit his face and he raised his chin in her direction and waved. Melody's stomach flipped.

"Is he waving at us?" Denise's voice carried anticipation and hope.

"Yeah, I think so." Melody hesitated before sharing. "I met him yesterday actually. His name's Zach." She saw Denise's jaw drop and after a little giggle escaped her, said, "You'd better shut your mouth before you catch a fly... or a lightning bug."

"But how did you? I mean where—?"

"On the beach. The girl he's with dropped out of their volleyball game, and I filled in."

"Damn! Well, I'm calling dibs!"

"Looks like someone beat you to it, Dee."

"Yeah, but when he gets tired of her, I'll be in line, so don't you go falling for him."

Too late...

5 Rejoining

After that night around the campfire, Melody did her best to put Zach out of her mind, but she was still determined to stop brooding. *Life is too short.* Besides she knew her father wouldn't want her moping like Eeyore. He always said God wanted us to be joyful. She would choose the exuberance of Tigger!

In the days that followed, there were many volleyball games on the beach, and it wasn't long before Melody learned a little secret about Anne Marie. She wasn't Zach's girlfriend; she was his sister. His twin sister!

Melody toyed with the idea of not telling Denise but thought better of it and decided to share the news. So, the morning games on the beach often had one more girl joining in. Melody wasn't sure she had ever seen her best friend so excited about being on the beach. Denise was typically more of a pool girl and not particularly athletic.

"C'mon, Dee! You can be on our team."

Denise was off her towel and on her feet before the last words were out of Zach's mouth. She winked at Melody who was already standing by the net, and Melody laughed even though a part of her wanted to cry.

"Hot damn, Mel!" Denise whispered.

There wasn't time for any more conversation as someone from the other side of the net sent the ball in their direction. Denise made an unsuccessful effort, but Melody dove and set the ball so Zach could slam it over the net.

"Good one!" Zach yelled with a quick high-five to Mel.

Denise shot her a glance Melody couldn't quite decipher, but by the end of the game, she had the impression her friend was not happy with her.

"What's wrong, Dee?"

"Nothing."

Melody found that hard to believe as her friend headed up the beach without another word. "Denise, hold up! Why don't you come up to the house? Maybe go for a swim?"

Reaching the spot where she'd left her towel, Denise grabbed it and turned to face Melody and the rest of the kids talking and laughing in groups of two or three, but Zach wasn't in any of those groups. He stood alone a few feet behind Melody.

"No, that's okay. I think someone is waiting for you."

Melody looked over her shoulder and spotted Zach smiling, watching her. She wanted to hang out with him more than anything. After all, she could see he was waiting for her... but her best friend needed her. She could feel it.

After a struggle of mere seconds which felt much longer, Melody gave Zach a quick smile and wave and chased after her friend. Melody's slight hesitation had apparently signaled Denise that she was going to stay on the beach, so she had begun to trudge through the sand.

Melody ran kicking sand behind her and called out as she passed her BFF. "Race ya!" She kept running without looking back, hoping she was being followed. Seconds later, out of the corner of her eye, she caught a glimpse of Denise, and the two girls dissolved into laughter as they crossed the dune and reached the edge of the Patterson's property.

Denise touched the fence first—and Melody had no intention of admitting she'd let her friend win—then the two of them headed up to the pool area.

"All right, you won that one, but I'll beat you in the pool." Melody's competitive spirit wouldn't allow her to do otherwise, not even to make her friend feel better.

Denise accepted the challenge—and lost. But Melody knew she was used to that and wouldn't mind. Before long they both collapsed onto a couple of the blue chaises facing the sun, laughing and talking and seeming to forget the earlier concerns.

"I've missed this," Denise said jolting upright.

It took a moment before Melody understood. "Yeah, me too. I guess I didn't realize how much I missed it until now. I suppose I've been a bit of a drag ever since... ever since my dad... since he died."

"Sorry, I shouldn't have said anything."

"Why not? You're right. I've been moping around for so long, and it doesn't change anything. I'm sorry."

"No one blames you, yanno? I mean, your dad was great. Everyone liked him a lot. I wish my father was more like him."

Melody understood, considering how Mr. Henley had always acted when she was around, and Denise said that was mild compared to his rants when it was just her and her mom. It was probably the alcohol that made him so surly. Denise had often told her how nasty and insulting he was to her mother when he was drinking, and how sullen and apologetic he'd be the next day. Yet the drinking was getting worse, and so was his disposition.

Talking about him was so depressing, Denise changed the subject which inevitably came back to the topic they'd both hesitated to broach.

"So do you like him?" Denise was leaning on one elbow watching for Melody's response.

"Who?"

"Ha-ha, very funny. You know who."

Denise and Melody had been best friends ever since they met in fourth grade when the Pattersons moved to the area, and Melody didn't want to let anything ruin their friendship... not even Zach.

Nobody's worth that, Melody thought as she looked longingly toward the beach.

Should I be honest? "Well, he's definitely cute, and..."

"Yep, that's what I thought. OMG, why didn't you say so?"

6 ᒪIFE CHANGES

August

Judy Patterson was relieved to see her youngest daughter at last getting back to her old self. Chelsea had grieved of course, and they all still had their teary moments, but it was Melody who had worried her most. The changes in her personality that lingered and her refusal to talk about her father were concerning.

Over the summer, though, Melody had begun to rejoin her friends on the beach and had even taken a parttime job at "Books and Things"—the little bookstore in town now owned by Zach's parents, Walt and Cindy Farley—and Judy was pretty sure the owners' son had more to do with her choice than did the actual job. Judy decided both her daughters would be all right... but would she?

She could shut out the loneliness by staying busy. Working four days a week at a nearby restaurant was a distraction that kept her from dwelling on the loss of her husband, and when she returned home, there were always chores to be done.

Chelsea was a huge help with meals, and Judy was glad her oldest daughter shared her love of cooking. From the time she was little more than a toddler, Chelsea had begged to dump ingredients in the bowl, stir the cake batter, and of course, lick the spoon. Now she had developed her skills to the point there was little more her mother could teach her. She was becoming a regular little Julia Child... or Rachel Ray. At least a couple of times a week Judy would come home to the smell of some fresh baked delight.

So, it wasn't a terrible surprise when Judy discovered her oldest daughter's dream was not to go to college following high school, but to go to culinary school and maybe someday have her own restaurant. Judy thought it was a wonderful idea, and since her husband's death, finances were a little tighter so it relieved the worry of college tuition at least for one of her girls. Not that finances were really a concern. Ken Patterson had insured their future with a substantial life insurance policy as well as the assets they had accumulated. Judy didn't have to work at all for them to continue to live in their home on the beach—now totally paid for— and not change their lifestyle.

No, Judy didn't work in order to survive financially. She worked in order to survive emotionally. Her life had become a puzzle missing a vital piece.

And those busy days at the restaurant were the perfect solution. However, when Judy closed her bedroom door at night and crawled into her empty bed, grief and loneliness were all that lay by her side.

It was mid-August when she noticed Sterling Blair in a new way.

The widower had entered her life for the first time not long after Christmas. She had often seen him and his daughter at church. Carol, his only child, was in her first year at Harvard, so he sat alone in his pew near the front each Sunday where he used to watch Carol singing in the choir. It had always been just the two of them, as far as Judy could remember, and with Carol in the choir loft, Judy could only remember Sterling sitting alone. But somehow, he looked much lonelier now.

One hot Sunday morning, Sterling had been in his typical spot when Judy and her daughters approached their usual pew, but Judy stopped short. Their spot was not empty and waiting. A family of five—obviously visitors or new to the church—sat in the place typically left open for them. Judy and the girls had turned back to look for another available pew when Sterling smiled up at them, slid over, and indicated there was room for them beside him. Judy smiled, graciously accepted, and slid onto the bench ahead of her girls.

At the point in the service where congregants greet each other—often with an embrace—Judy hugged her oldest daughter, then as Chelsea turned to hug her little sister, Judy turned and accepted a hug from Sterling. It seemed a very normal and natural thing to do.

What wasn't normal, or natural, was what Judy felt when they hugged. They may have held it for a second or two longer than most. *What was that all about?* Judy wondered. It had been so long since she'd felt a man's warm embrace that she didn't want to let go. She shook the feeling off, but the memory lingered long after they had said goodbye and shaken hands at the end of the service. Although she tried to deny it, Judy felt something again when their hands touched, and she believed from his expression, Sterling Blair felt it too.

The following Sunday morning, Judy had dressed with more care and suffered a bit of disappointment as she followed her girls into their usual pew. The family of strangers were sitting on the other side of the church this week. She pushed aside the tinge of disappointment and focused her mind on more appropriate thoughts for the setting.

She looked over at the newcomers. *I really must introduce myself to them and make them feel welcomed. That's what Ken would have done.*

It was coming up on the anniversary of her husband's death, and thinking about him now left no room for thoughts of Sterling Blair other than to feel a pang of guilt. The organist began playing the first hymn—one of Ken's favorites, "Crown Him with Many Crowns"—and Judy's throat tightened. This one was going to be rough.

Judy hadn't thought much about Mr. Blair until the following spring when she was delighted to see he was not alone. Carol had come home for spring-break. His pleasure at having her, even if it was just for a while, showed in his smile and in his eyes.

The following Sunday, she noticed a difference in his demeanor once again. Judy wondered how she would feel when her nest emptied, leaving her alone in that big house by the sea. Apprehension made her heart go out to the man in the pew behind her.

She saw Sterling on the parking lot after church that day, and impulsively approached. "Hi there. I wanted to tell you, your daughter looked wonderful last week. You must be so proud."

"Indeed, I am." Gratitude lit his face. "As I'm sure you are of your two beautiful daughters. We are blessed, aren't we?"

Judy agreed, then unable to think of anything else, she turned back toward her car.

"Wait."

Judy spun back around at the sound of Sterling's voice.

"I don't mean to be presumptuous, but I recently joined a group, Parents Without Partners. I don't know if you'd be interested, but it's a fun group. We go to dinner once a month. It's a chance to be something more than just a parent and to get out and relax and laugh with friends, with your peers. We laugh a lot; it's great medicine. If you ever think you might be interested, I can give you more information."

Judy thanked him but protested that with her busy schedule, she couldn't possibly find the time.

Parents *Without* Partners. She hated the very sound of it. It put such a loud exclamation point on the fact that her husband was gone. Gone forever. She had no one. *No! Not for me.*

However, on the ride home, listening to her daughters' animated chatter, she wondered, *Would it really be so terrible to have a social life, to have a little fun?* But how could she, with Ken gone forever?

7 Unexpected

"So exactly what is it Mom's doing tonight?" Melody sat at the island watching her sister busily chop broccoli and bell peppers and toss ingredients into the stir-fry she was preparing for their dinner.

Chelsea paused and screwed up her face. "I think it's something about people without partners." She added a generous helping of shrimp into the wok and seasoned them with salt and pepper.

Melody didn't like the idea at all. "What's the point? She has us. I mean, what partner? Is she talking about Dad?"

"Duh! Grab a couple plates. This is almost ready." Chelsea removed the pink shrimp and added the chopped broccoli, peppers, and sugar snap peas to the hot sesame oil. "What's your problem with Mom going out? I think it will be good for her to spend time with people her age. You wanna get the rice?"

"Sure." Melody watched Chelsea add garlic and ginger and drew in the fragrance, wondering how her sister had gotten to be such a good cook. Melody always enjoyed the results but had no desire to emulate her.

Chelsea whisked together soy sauce, cornstarch, lime juice, brown sugar and a pinch of red pepper flakes and added them to the skillet, then returned the shrimp to the wok and cooked it for a couple more minutes until it was heated through.

After filling their plates, the girls carried them to the big island—they never used the dining room when it was just the two of them—and Melody poured them each a cup of tea, which Chelsea insisted was necessary with Chinese stir-fry.

"This smells so good, Chels. No, Star, this isn't for you." Melody had learned to ignore those begging eyes—most of the time—and she dug into her sister's Chinese delight. "Shazam! That's good."

"Wait 'til you taste what I baked for dessert. It's a ginger layer cake with wine poached pears and cream cheese frosting."

Melody glanced over at the dessert on the counter. "It looks amazing. I don't see why you have to go to culinary school next year. You already know how to make all kinds of fancy stuff."

Chelsea put her chopsticks down. "Seriously? I mean thanks, but I don't know anything compared to those real chefs like Alex and Giada."

"You and your foodies." Melody rolled her eyes. "But there are plenty of places you could go here in the states." She couldn't imagine what it would be like with her sister on the other side of the Atlantic... and then there were the changes in her mother. *Everything keeps changing.*

"Sure there are, but Melody, just think of it... Paris! And maybe you can come visit."

Melody saw the excitement in her sister's eyes, and she wanted to be happy for her, but it was hard when she thought of being alone. With Chelsea away and their mom working—and now socializing—Melody could feel the impending loneliness closing in on her already.

Chelsea's dessert did not disappoint. "I'm stuffed!" Melody dropped her fork on the plate and leaned back in her seat holding her belly. "Wait 'til Mom tries this. She's gonna love it. When do you think she'll be home anyway?"

"I'm not sure. I think they were having dinner at Bethany Blues. Probably won't be too late. Why?"

"No reason. Just wondered." Melody wasn't sure why it bothered her, but she had a niggling feeling that wouldn't let go.

"Hey, did Mom tell you Mr. Sipe was asking about you? He wanted to know if you could help them out this year."

Howard Sipe, the choir director at Christ Church had approached Melody earlier in the year about rejoining the choir, but she hadn't been ready then, and she wasn't sure if she was ready now.

"He said the alto section is getting along, but since Carol Blair went off to college, he could really use you in the soprano section. They miss your voice, Mel."

"No, I guess she forgot to tell me. I'll think about it." *Maybe it's time.* Singing had been Melody's first love since she was a toddler. Now she would finally get to sing soprano, and her voice had been silent for too long. "Did I tell you Mrs. Cox wants me to try out for the lead in our school musical?"

"What?" Chelsea rushed over to hug her sister. "That's amazing!"

"Well, I didn't get the part yet."

"But you will! You know you will. Your voice is amazing. You got that from Dad." Chelsea's final words had a sobering effect on Melody, but she knew it was true.

Her mother and sister could carry a tune, but there was nothing particularly special about their voices, while Melody had shown her special gift by the time she was in preschool. By fourth grade her parents had enrolled her in voice lessons, and now Melody could see no future that didn't include singing.

***

Melody didn't hear her mother come in about an hour later, so she was startled by her sudden appearance in the bedroom doorway.

"Hey Mel, your sister and I are going to watch a Hallmark movie. Do you want to join us?"

"No thanks." Melody had been lost in thought, but she knew she wasn't in the mood for one of those sappy Christmas movies her mother loved to watch. They were all pretty much the same anyway. Small town, Christmas carols, snow, a troubled romance, and of course, a Christmas miracle and happily ever after.

The only Christmas miracle that could make her happy was her father sitting in his big brown chair reading from the Gospel of Luke on Christmas Eve. Nope, no happily ever after here.

"Okay, but if you change your mind... we're making popcorn. Oh, and you could have another piece of your sister's delicious pear cake."

"Okay, thanks. I might be down then."

It wasn't the cake—as luscious as that was—but the smell of popcorn that drew her away from the sad aria playing in her ears and the memories haunting her mind. She was greeted with smiles, and Judy Patterson patted the spot on the sofa next to her.

Grabbing a handful of the offered popcorn which had been sprinkled with parmesan cheese, her favorite, she settled in on the couch next to her mother. The movie had the usual small-town setting filled with smiling people, snow on the ground, and everyone planning for the big day.

During the first commercial break, Judy asked if Melody had given any thought to helping Mr. Sipe out by singing in the choir this year. Obviously, she and Chelsea had been talking.

"I don't know. Maybe."

"He said they really need you." Judy patted her daughter's knee. "You have such a beautiful, strong voice. I know I'd love to see you up there again. I miss that."

Yeah, but Dad won't be there. It will never be the same.

Melody was glad when the movie resumed, and her mother's focus returned to it. However, her own attention had been diverted, and all she could think of now was the upcoming holiday... their second Christmas without her father. Maybe it was time to stop wallowing and revisit her dream. It was time to find her voice again.

On the next commercial, Melody kissed her mother on the cheek. "I think I'm going to go read for a while."

"Oh, don't you like this one?" Chelsea asked pointing to the TV.

Melody laughed. "They're pretty much all the same, aren't they? And I'm kind of tired." She paused before adding, "But I think I will go ahead and sing this year."

Her mother jumped up from the sofa and gave her a quick hug. "I'm so glad, honey."

Melody couldn't help wondering if it was her news about rejoining the choir or her mother's time with this Parents Without Partners group that had added such life to her eyes.

***

With Christmas still a few weeks away Melody was able to attend a couple choir rehearsals, and it didn't take long before all their voices blended into the beautiful sound of the Hallelujah Chorus.

Those few weeks flew by, and on Christmas Eve, joined by their mother, Melody and Chelsea trimmed the tree, putting on all the traditional ornaments. It was Judy who placed the one of her and their father. The silence in the few seconds that followed was filled with emotion, but Judy swiped away the unbidden tears, laughing a bit nervously.

"All right, enough of that. I think it's time we bundle up and head to the church so you have time to get ready."

Yet there would be more tears. Melody donned her choir robes and joined the rest of the singers in their candlelight procession. The church was filled beyond capacity—as it always was on Christmas Eve—and the service was beautiful. It wasn't until the triumphant singing of the Hallelujah Chorus that she glanced down at her mother and sister sitting in the third pew as they had for so many Christmases, and she saw Chelsea smiling and singing along. But her mother wasn't singing. Melody noticed her mother's lips squeezed tight as she dabbed at her eyes.

Before getting caught up in those emotions, Melody forced her attention back to the choir director and finishing the anthem. Following the last notes of the song, she knew it had been perfect...

except for the one missing piece... the sound of one beautiful baritone.

8 Choices

Judy looked forward to the monthly dinner meetings of her Parents Without Partners group, leaving work and worry behind while laughing and having fun with new friends. Since Sterling had invited her to join the group, it had been quite natural for him to sit with her the first time she attended.

In the months that followed, they continued to sit together at each restaurant, and their friendship blossomed. Judy enjoyed Sterling's company and the comfortable conversations they shared, yet she was surprised when after the April dinner, he asked her if she'd like to have dinner with him one evening. Not dinner with the group. Just the two of them. Like a date.

Her hesitation before answering spurred Sterling to add, "That's okay. I didn't mean to overstep."

"No! You didn't. I, I was just surprised... but yes, sure. Why not?" she said grinning, realizing she really did like the idea. *But will the girls?*

Judy felt a twinge of guilt at the idea of going on a "date" when Ken had only been gone two years. Still, at forty-three, she was too young to spend the rest of her life alone. Besides, this was one date—two people sharing a meal. It's not like she was planning to marry the guy.

Judy wrestled with these conflicting thoughts on the whole ride home, but by the time she pulled into the garage, she'd decided. She would have dinner with Sterling Blair, and she would not feel guilty about it.

Still, the following Saturday afternoon as she broached the subject, she wondered how the girls would react. She decided to ease into it.

"What are you girls doing tonight?"

"Bobby and I are going over to his sister's house to have dinner with her and her husband." Chelsea had been dating Bob Longo for a couple months and would be taking him to prom. Although she professed to like him a lot, she wasn't ready to get serious with anyone before heading off to culinary school abroad.

"How about you, Mel? Do you have any plans?" Judy hoped she would answer in the affirmative.

"It's so nice out, a bunch of us decided to play mini-golf this afternoon then grab something to eat after. Yeah, so I won't be here for dinner. Sorry. Hate to leave you all alone."

"Oh, I won't be alone." Judy took a deep breath. "I'm actually going out to dinner tonight too."

Two heads snapped around as her daughters' faces tossed out the unspoken question. It was Chelsea who asked.

"By yourself? I mean, who are you having dinner with?"

"My friend, Sterling… Sterling Blair. You know, the man who invited me to join the Parents Without Partners group? We thought we'd have dinner tonight." Judy saw a look of surprise on Chelsea's face and Melody's eyes widened.

The few seconds before anyone spoke seemed endless to Judy.

"That's cool." Chelsea was the first to speak.

Judy didn't miss the disapproving look on her youngest daughter's face before she replied, "Yeah… cool. Okay, well I've got to get ready. Zach will be here to pick me up soon."

Melody made a quick exit, and Chelsea looked sheepish.

"Don't worry, Mom. She was just taken by surprise. I guess we both were… but she'll be all right." Chelsea gave her mother a peck on the cheek. "Besides, I think she's pretty goo-goo eyed over Zach lately, so I wouldn't worry about it."

"Thanks, sweetie." Judy appreciated her oldest daughter's efforts at smoothing away any discomfort. She wondered, though, if Melody *was* upset—Chelsea too, for that matter—but then decided she wouldn't let her daughters' opinions ruin an evening she was looking forward to spending with Sterling, a good friend.

Melody and Chelsea both left before Judy was dressed and ready to leave for the restaurant. Sterling had offered to pick her up, but since that felt way too much like a date, and she wasn't sure how the girls would react, she had suggested she meet him there.

Checking her appearance in the mirror, Judy approved of her selection of the lavender dress and matching sweater. The three-quarter-inch silver-leaf earrings were the perfect length to go with her new short haircut, so she tidied her auburn locks, checked her makeup, and headed for the bedroom door. The picture hanging on her bedroom wall—*their* bedroom wall—caught her eye. It was a photo from their wedding day twenty years ago... the happiest day of her life—well that and the birth of her first child.

Judy touched her husband's face in the picture, and spoke to him. *I love you, Ken. I love you so much...*

Then, she hurried from the room, got her things, and left to meet another man for the first date of her new life.

Surprised at how utterly relaxed she was with Sterling, by the end of the evening, Judy knew this wouldn't be the last dinner the two of them would share. It felt good to be with him, to talk, to laugh, to be alive. There were none of the fireworks she'd experienced with Ken when they were young, but there was a quiet comfort like aromatherapy or a glass of fine wine.

They lingered over dessert and talked until their waitress had returned several times to ask if they'd like anything else.

"I think she's trying to get rid of us," Judy said.

"I think you're right," Sterling murmured with a wink, "but I hate to see the evening end. This has been fun. I hope we can do it again sometime."

Judy gazed into his brown eyes filled with warmth and replied, "I hope so too. And sometime soon."

By the time Sterling had walked Judy to her car, they had already made plans for their next *date*.

9 When the Curtain Falls

May 2017

The day of her first performance in the high-school musical came at last, and Melody was surprisingly calm as the curtains opened and she looked out on the crowd in the auditorium. She didn't see individual faces, merely a sea of smiles as they anxiously awaited the first song.

Then, when she opened her mouth to sing, the notes flowed as though she were a finely tuned instrument. Ken Patterson had once told Melody her voice was like the song of a perfectly tuned violin... an instrument that touches the soul... a gift from God.

But on this night, being so well rehearsed and in possession of such talent, she wasn't thinking about that. She simply thrilled at being on stage performing. She knew this was exactly where she was supposed to be... and when the curtain finally closed to thunderous applause, she felt exhilarated and proud of herself.

Melody scanned the crowd during their curtain calls and spotted Chelsea. Her boyfriend, Bob, was sitting to her right, and to her left sat Judy who was beaming with pride. Melody's heart soared until she saw the man on her mother's left. It was Sterling Blair. It should have been her dad.

Melody swallowed the sudden lump in her throat and kept smiling and bowing until the curtains closed for the last time. As she turned to dash off stage, she found herself in an unanticipated bearhug from her good-looking costar.

"You were great, Mel!" Zach lifted her up and swept her in a circle until they were both laughing with joy. Then he kissed her... right there in front of everyone. She heard a few ohs and ahs from their fellow cast members, but then everyone was hastening off stage to change and meet their families and friends.

The warmth flowing into Melody's cheeks at the unexpected kiss and the excitement she felt were both new to her. Although she'd had a crush on Zach for a while, she'd been afraid to believe the feeling was mutual. They had been hanging out together lately, but he had never indicated he felt more than friendship for her. The man sitting next to her mother in the audience now forgotten, Melody could think of nothing but the boy still touching her arm and saying something. *Oh Lord, what did he just say?*

"So, what do you say?"

He was looking at her expectantly. Melody's mind scrambled, and she knew she had to say something... but what?

His next words solved the mystery. "Hey, if you have other plans to eat with your family or something, it's all right. I understand."

"No! I mean, I don't have any special plans... at least nothing I can't get out of."

"Great! I'll tell the others and meet you out front."

Zach took off running and an exhilarated though flustered Melody hurried to change and tell her mother and sister she was going *somewhere* with some friends.

They were waiting for her in front of the auditorium when she got there, and as soon as they saw her, all four began clapping.

"Bravo! You were great, honey!"

Melody could see the pride in her mother's eyes. Sterling Blair stood quietly by her side, smiling.

"Yeah," Chelsea said taking her turn to hug her—not something they did often but seeming quite natural on this occasion—and grinning from ear to ear. "You killed it. Look out, Broadway, here she comes!"

Melody laughed at her sister's comment secretly hoping she was right. That was her dream. Ever since her father had taken her to see her first Broadway show, she had known that was what she was meant to do.

"Oh, these are for you." Judy took the flowers from Sterling and handed them to her. "We all thought a star like you deserved flowers." As she handed the bouquet to Melody, she placed a hand on her daughter's cheek. "I'm sure Daddy is looking down right now, and he's so very proud of you."

Melody looked at her mother through a sudden blur. "Thanks, Mom." She dabbed the tears away and remembered Zach was waiting for her when Chelsea spoke.

"So, let's all go get something to eat to celebrate, huh?"

"Oh, I'm sorry. I, I didn't know... I mean I didn't realize you'd want to... I mean I kind of told a bunch of the cast members I'd go out with them after." She glanced out the big glass window and saw Zach waiting.

After a short, awkward pause that seemed much longer to Melody than it was, her mother broke the silence. "Hey, that's fine. You should celebrate with your friends. You all did such a wonderful job."

Although her mother was letting her off the hook, Melody felt conflicted and a bit guilty. Yet the idea of going out with Zach had a stronger pull than going to dinner with her mother and a man who was *not* her father. She apologized again.

"Hey, go, have fun, Mel. But don't eat too much. We can have a treat when you get home." Chelsea winked when she said it, so Melody knew she'd baked something special.

After more hugs and saying a hasty goodbye to Chelsea, Bob, her mother and Mr. Blair, Melody dashed outside where Zach was waiting patiently.

"There you are!"

"Sorry! I had to talk to the family. They kind of thought we'd go out after."

"Oh, well if you want—" Zach looked disappointed.

"No! I mean, they're cool. We're gonna have dessert later when I get home. Let's go. I'm starving." Melody still wasn't sure where they were going or who else would be there, but it didn't matter. She was on a *date* with her costar, Zach Farley!

10 A Cookie's Truth

"So, Mom, what are you going to do? Bobby suggested we could get burgers or something."

Judy glanced at Sterling who shrugged and smiled.

"Tell you what, Chels, why don't you and Bobby go ahead, and Mr. Blair and I will see you back at the house later." She looked from her daughter to Sterling, both of whom looked agreeable. "Okay, that's settled. See you later!" Judy wasn't displeased at this latest development. Quiet time alone with Sterling was rare, and she found she enjoyed those times more and more.

"I'm thinking Italian or Chinese sounds better than burgers," Sterling said after Chelsea and her boyfriend took off.

"How about we do Chinese carryout and take it back to my place?" Judy liked Chinese food, but even more, she liked the idea of the two of them spending quiet time at home. Sterling had never been to her house except to pick her up for dinner, so this felt like a next step to her, a next step she was finally prepared to take.

They took the food straight to the kitchen when they got back to the Patterson house, and Judy set places at the island and dished the food into bowls. Sterling had objected, saying it wasn't necessary to make more dirty dishes, but it was Judy's habit to do it this way. Although a guest, Sterling insisted on helping, and when Judy turned around and saw him scooping fried rice into the bowl she'd provided, she stopped short.

How many times had Ken stood at that very spot helping her dish up Sunday dinner? She missed him so much in that moment, she felt like she should send Sterling away.

"Are you all right?"

Startled by his voice, her head jerked up, and she recovered her smile. "Yes, why?"

"I don't know. You just looked kind of distracted. Never mind."

"Sorry. You know what? There's no reason I shouldn't tell you." Judy put napkins by the plates then, without looking at her *date*, she tried to explain. "When I saw you standing there, it... it reminded me of how my husband used to help me in the kitchen. I'm sorry."

"You don't need to apologize. You have no reason to be sorry. You lost the man you loved. The man you shared your life with." He moved toward her, then stopped about two feet away. "It's been nearly ten years since I lost Jojo, and I still have my moments."

Sterling's caring face blurred before Judy's eyes as she lost the battle to fight back the tears. She grabbed a napkin to blot away those that trickled down her cheeks and smiled up at him. "Okay, enough of that. Let's eat. I, for one, am famished, and this smells so good."

Sterling put his hands on her arms, pulled her toward him, and kissed her gently on the forehead. "Sounds good to me."

The conversation shifted as Judy guided it to one of their favorite subjects, their children. They talked about Melody's gifted ability to sing and how well she'd done in the musical; they talked about Carol's progress at Harvard and how she had joined their prestigious choir; finally, they talked about Chelsea's wonderful baking skills and how much they were looking forward to digging into today's dessert.

"In the meantime, how 'bout one of these fortune cookies?" Sterling held out the two Pac-man shaped cookies for Judy to choose from.

"Sure, I know they can't compare to my daughter's dessert, but they are fun." Judy cracked open her cookie and took out the slip of paper. Reading it blew her mind. "Change is inevitable," she read aloud, raising her eyes to meet Sterling's gaze.

Neither said anything until Sterling broke the spell by cracking open his own cookie. "Flattery will go far tonight." He chuckled. "Well, I certainly hope so, and by the way, have I told you what a lovely smile you have?"

Judy joined in his laughter knowing her cheeks must have pinkened with the compliment. "Thank you." This time it was Judy who broke the silence. "I guess I'd better clear all this away to make room for Chelsea's grand dessert presentation.

They had put the empty containers in the trash, leftovers in the fridge, and dishes in the dishwasher when Chelsea and Bobby bopped in.

"Isn't Melody back yet?" Chelsea asked. "Mmm, smells Chinese in here."

"No, not yet." Judy gave her oldest daughter a hug.

"Should we dig into dessert now or wait for her?" Chelsea looked at Bob. "I think this guy is drooling."

"It's up to you all of course, but I'm pretty stuffed after my General Tso's chicken." Sterling rubbed his belly. "I can wait."

With everyone in agreement, they moved to the family room where Bobby and Chelsea plopped onto one end of the sofa, and Judy sat on the other.

Not wanting to squeeze in next to her, Sterling took a seat in the big chair nearby. Judy gasped on seeing him in her husband's chair. She wished she had indicated another spot for him and wondered if she should have offered him the couch, and she could have sat in one of the chairs. No one ever sat in *Ken's chair.*

"Hello! I'm home!" In another heartbeat, Melody stood in the doorway. The look of shock on her face said it all.

11 Shared Turmoil

$\mathcal{M}$elody was still walking on clouds when she got home. As if the success of their musical hadn't been enough, their after-the-show celebration had been the icing on her happiness cake.

But seeing Sterling Blair sitting in her father's chair was as deflating as a balloon landing on a cactus.

She clamped her mouth shut as soon as she realized her jaw had dropped, but when she glanced at her mother, it was obvious her shock hadn't gone unnoticed.

Judy Patterson jumped to her feet and rushed to hug her daughter. "I'm sorry," she whispered in Melody's ear. Then aloud she said, "Here's our star! Oh Mel, I'm so proud of you. You were wonderful!"

"Thanks, Mom." Melody appreciated the time her mother had provided for her to compose herself. Everyone had gotten to their feet to give her another round of applause. "Okay, you guys. Chill." Melody laughed.

"Well, I made a special dessert for the star. No, not you, Star!" Their faithful four-legged pooch had come running at the sound of her name. "Here," Chelsea said, giving the dog a treat from her special jar. "I hope you saved a little room, Mel."

"Are you kidding? I always have room for your creations. What are we having?"

"Nothing too fancy. Just your favorite."

"Boston cream pie? Bring it on!"

"Why don't we all move to the dining room for dessert?" Judy guided everyone in the right direction. "Where did you all go for dinner? Was it the whole cast?"

Melody told them all about their after-party while they enjoyed Chelsea's Boston Cream Pie, but she didn't mention the kiss. That was too special. That was hers and hers alone, at least until she talked to her best friend.

Half an hour later Chelsea and Bob left to go for a walk on the beach, leaving Melody feeling awkward and unsure what to do. Chelsea wouldn't want her sister tagging along with her and her boyfriend, and Melody had no desire to sit in the family room with her mother and the interloper.

"I think I'm going to go call Denise."

Once in her room, Melody wandered over to her window and looked out at the full moon shining in the cloudless sky. The only cloud was in Melody's mind as she struggled with the negative feelings she was having toward her mother's new friend.

She didn't want to hate Mr. Blair—or Sterling, as he'd said she could call him—and she didn't actually. Yet there was no denying her shock and resentment when she saw him sitting in her father's chair.

Melody pulled her cell phone out of her pocket and hit her best friend's number.

"Hey Mel, what's up?" Denise sounded surprised to hear from her. "Is something wrong?"

"No, can't a friend call her bestie without anything being wrong?" Both girls laughed.

"Sure, but I thought we'd about covered everything when we were together, like an hour ago."

"Yeah, that was so fun, and Mitch was looking all goo-goo-eyed at you. I think he's in love."

"All right, Mel, knock it off. You know he's not my type. But Zach seems to be your type."

Melody thought about that and hoped Denise was right and that she was *his* type.

"So, what's going on? Was that guy still there when you got home?"

"Yeah... and he's still here."

"You sound so bummed. Don't let it get to you."

"But Dee, he was sitting in Dad's chair!" There was silence on the other end. "You don't understand. I mean, no one sits there. It... it's just wrong. I don't know why Mom let him sit there."

"That really sucks. I'm sorry, Mel."

Melody thought her friend sounded sincere, but wondered how she could possibly understand. She still had a father, and besides, she and her dad weren't close. All that man did was work... and drink. He was hardly ever home, and it wasn't very pleasant when he was. No wonder Denise and her mother were like best friends. It had almost always been just the two of them.

"But at least you had a good dad. Mine is... never mind."

"What's going on? Did something happen?"

"I might as well tell you. I was gonna wait cuz I didn't want to spoil your day, but it sounds like it's already been kind of spoiled by this Blair guy."

"What's wrong?"

"Dad left. Mom kicked him out."

"What? Are you serious?"

"Yep. Mom told him to pack his stuff while we were at the show and to be gone when we got home. She didn't tell me until I got home cuz she didn't want to upset me."

"Holy crap! You gotta be kidding! Do you want me to come over?" Melody forgot all about the man downstairs for the moment.

"No. It's getting late, and right now Mom needs me. I think we're better off without him, but he left us a crappy note saying how sorry he was and promising all kinds of BS, and now she's a wreck."

Melody heard the break in her best friend's voice and knew it was all bravado. She wished there was something she could do to help... but what?

"Okay... well, you know I'm here for you. Call me later if you wanna talk."

After hearing her best friend's news, Melody needed to talk to someone about it. She opened the bedroom door and listened for voices. She didn't hear a sound and, hoping that meant Mr. Blair was gone, she ventured to the family room from which she could hear the TV.

He was still there and sitting next to her mother on the couch. Glad he wasn't in her father's chair, but *not* happy to see him next to Mom, Melody turned to leave, but not in time.

"Mel, come on in. Did you want to watch TV?"

"No, Mom. I wanted to talk to you about something, but it can wait."

As she turned to leave once again, it was Sterling's voice that stopped her. "Don't go, Melody" She saw him check his watch. "I think I'd better be off now, so I'll get out of your way."

Judy tried to object, then walked him to the door when he insisted he was tired and said he'd call her.

Melody plopped onto the couch and put her head on her mother's shoulder when she returned.

"What's wrong, hon?"

"It's Denise."

"Oh no... what is it? Is she all right?"

Melody heard the concern in her mother's voice. Denise had been spending time at their house for so many years, she was almost like a third daughter to Judy Patterson, as Melody was to Mrs. Henley.

"Her father is an asshat."

"Melody!"

"Sorry, but it's true."

"I know you don't think much of him, but that's uncalled for."

"Really?" Melody pulled back and glared at her mother. "Well, you don't know what he did. I think it's totally called for. He's so mean when he drinks—and he drinks All. The. Time. So, Mrs. Henley *finally* sent him packing. Instead of coming to watch Dee in the show, he used that time to pack up and leave... didn't even say goodbye to her." Melody jumped to her feet. "Oh yeah, and then he left some kind of note with all kinds of promises and stuff and made her mom feel guilty." Melody headed for the door but turned back long enough to add, "So not only is he an asshat, he's a liar and a creep."

"Melody, wait!" Judy called after her daughter as she headed out of the room. "Melody Ann!"

12 ᴇɴᴅɪɴɢꜱ & ʙᴇɢɪɴɴɪɴɢꜱ

June

In the month since Melody's high school musical, Judy had noticed the return of her youngest daughter's sullenness and vast mood swings and found them concerning, but in this moment her focus was on her older daughter. Anticipation grew as the names were called and each senior walked across the stage, took their diploma from the principal, shook her hand, and then turned to grin at their cheering families.

Jennifer Ann Miller... Thomas Earl Moss... James Lee Parker... and then, Chelsea Elizabeth Patterson.

Judy's heart swelled with pride as she watched her daughter accept her diploma, and she looked through a haze of tears thinking of someone else also watching from heaven.

Our first born, Kenny... she's growing up. Oh God, she's ready to leave the nest.

"Are you crying, Mom?" Judy realized Melody was staring at her as Chelsea exited the stage to return to her seat. Her younger daughter chuckled. "Yeah, I'm proud of her too."

Judy patted Melody's knee. "And so is your dad."

She didn't miss the sudden sadness that crossed her daughter's face, but it was quickly replaced by a brave smile and a whispered, "I know."

But Judy couldn't help thinking beyond the happiness of the day, realizing what was ahead. She wanted Chelsea to be happy and reach her goals, but the idea of her being an ocean away was agonizing.

Shaking it off, she forced herself to stay in the present. This was a day to celebrate, not a day for melancholy. So, feelings of gloom were set aside while the celebration ensued.

An hour later, friends and family gathered on the over-sized patio behind the Patterson house, and many of the younger crowd braved the pool even though it made Judy shiver to watch. Though it was heated, she knew the early June air off the ocean would be cool on their wet skin, but youth seemed immune to the cold. Judy knew some would even frolic in the ocean waves before assembling around the firepit when evening fell.

She was right, and as night fell, she pulled her pashmina tight and listened to the laughter drifting up from the firepit area. It was music to her ears, but it had a sad note since it would likely be the final melody from Chelsea's gang.

Glad for the distraction, Judy grabbed her vibrating phone and, seeing the call was from Sterling, put a smile in her voice.

"How are things going in Boston?" Judy knew her doldrums were accented by his absence, but his daughter, Carol, had invited him to come up and have dinner with her, her boyfriend, and the boyfriend's parents.

"Precisely as I'd expected." There was a chuckle in his voice. "I had no sooner gotten to her apartment than she was flashing the ring in my face." Sterling knew Carol's relationship with her fellow Harvard boyfriend was getting serious, and he had suspected this dinner was to announce an engagement, so he was right. "This Brad is stealing her away. Yep, my little girl is getting married… and soon."

Though he seemed to be making light of it, Judy knew he must be feeling the impending loss. Having his daughter away at Harvard was one thing, but knowing she would be leaving permanently was quite another.

"Well, what did you think of this guy, Brad, was it?"

"If he wasn't about to marry my daughter, I'd probably like him. I might not even be thinking about shooting him." He laughed again. "You know, he seems like a good kid… and the way he looks at Carol, there's no doubt he loves her. And I liked the guy's parents right away. All in all, I think she found a good man so I shouldn't worry."

"I know, but I would imagine it must be more difficult knowing your empty nest is going to be more permanent soon. Chelsea is just leaving for a year abroad, and I'm already feeling it."

"How was the graduation?"

Judy told him all about the ceremony, the pride she felt, and the fun all the kids were still having. "I feel like an old lady sitting here listening to them. Melody and her BFF went inside to watch a movie, so I'm sitting on the patio with Star as my only company." The dog's tail thumped in response, before she put her head down and closed her eyes once more. "And she's not much company."

The dog must have heard the insult because her eyes popped open and she got up and walked to the slider, looking back to be sure Judy got the message.

"Well, now she's leaving me too," Judy said getting up to let the dog in. "She'd rather be with Melody."

"Speaking of Melody, how's she doing?" It wasn't unusual for Sterling to ask since Judy often shared her concerns about her youngest.

"Up and down. I think she's struggling with Chelsea leaving even more than I am. Maybe it will give us a chance to get closer." Judy felt a twinge of guilt when she acknowledged the distance between them. "Since her father died, and they were so close, I think she's had a harder time than Chelsea who has always been my girl. Does that sound awful?"

"Not at all."

"I mean, I don't love her any less. She's my baby after all, but still, she was Daddy's little girl—his princess—and they shared so much... like their love of music."

"But I'm sure you must share some things too."

"Of course." Judy knew he was right but somehow couldn't think of a single thing. Then it hit her. "We do both love to run on the beach. Ken never was much of a runner. Neither was Chelsea." And she remembered how much she and Melody loved to swim laps in the morning, always ending with a race. She laughed a little when she shared this tidbit with Sterling, then realized with sadness how long it had been since she and her daughter had shared their old morning ritual.

The next morning, glad for the early sunshine as well as the heated pool, Judy waited for her youngest daughter. It was after 8:00 and the sun was already warming her skin when Melody appeared on the patio above the pool.

"Mom? What are you doing in your suit already?"

"I thought I'd better get my laps in. Your sister's baking skills are showing up on my hips. Want to join me?"

"Well, I, uh, I was heading for a run on the beach—"

"Oh, that sounds good. Mind if I join you?" Judy didn't miss her daughter's hesitation in responding and thought she was about to be rejected.

"Yeah, sure," Melody said, a slow smile brightening her face. "Let's go!"

It wasn't until about thirty minutes later, when they approached the new boy, Zach, who it seemed was becoming more than a friend, that she noticed her daughter's change in demeanor.

Melody waved and made a sharp turn to head back up the beach toward the house. Judy followed, full of curiosity.

"Hey, Mel!" Zach had stopped, and hands on hips asked, "Aren't you gonna play? Everybody should be here soon."

Melody looked at Zach, then at her mother.

Judy nodded. "Go ahead, sweetie."

"But you said you wanted to—"

"Don't be silly. You go ahead. I think I'm ready for a quick dip then I've got a good book waiting for me."

With a big grin, a genuine hug, and a *thanks Mom*, Melody turned and dashed back toward where Zach stood waiting.

Looks like my little girl has found someone she'd rather spend time with.

13 First Love

Melody loved her mom, and had always enjoyed their friendly competition, but she wondered why her mother suddenly wanted to spend time with her in the pool now. After all, they hadn't really done that since... when? Oh, since Dad died. The summer following his death neither one of them had been bent on racing and shenanigans.

Was this simply life getting back to normal?

But Melody didn't have much time to ponder the question before the others had gathered for the beach volleyball game they liked to get in before too many families arrived with their huge umbrellas in every shade of the rainbow.

There were already a few colorful umbrellas going up closer to the water's edge, but they all knew, with summer in full swing, there would be many more over the next hour or so. Blankets would be spread, and people would pull wagons loaded with towels, chairs, and coolers full of snacks and drinks for the day.

Melody remembered her own parents making the trek from the time she was a toddler until she was nine, and she remembered with delight how excited they'd been when they moved into their present home right on the beach. Though it was more than seven years ago, she still remembered the first time she'd seen the house like it was yesterday.

She was sure her eyes had nearly popped out of her head when she saw the pool and her daddy announced she could go swimming every single day now... and she nearly did from the first warm days of May until the mid-autumn chill made it too cold to swim even in their heated pool. The addition of the hot tub was nice, but her parents got a lot more use out of that than she or Chelsea.

"Melody!" The memory of her parents speaking in soft tones on quiet evenings in the hot tub, was interrupted by the sound of someone calling her name. It was Anne Marie, Zach's twin sister, who Melody had once thought to be his girlfriend. It was an honest mistake considering how close they were.

Zach and Anne Marie were the first fraternal twins Melody had ever met, and though they were as different in appearance as any brother and sister could be—one blue-eyed and fair-haired, the other a petite, striking brunette—they still seemed to share a special closeness unique to twins.

They appeared nearly inseparable. Wherever you saw Zach, you were sure to find Anne Marie nearby. It soon became apparent that Zach was the more outgoing twin while his "little sister" was extremely shy, so Melody was surprised to hear the shy twin calling her name.

"Hey, how's it going? Where's your brother?" Melody looked around but didn't see him, and she could always spot his sandy-colored hair if he was anywhere around.

"He asked me to tell you he can't make it this morning. Dad needs him to help with inventory. I think I'm going to head back and help too. They're pretty swamped with the summer crowd coming in."

"I have a better idea." Melody tried to hide her disappointment with an enthusiastic suggestion. "I'm supposed to work noon to four today anyway, so why don't I go in early, and you can stay and play?"

"Are you sure?"

Melody was more than sure as she dashed back toward the house to change and head for "Books and Things."

✳✳✳

"What are you doing here so early?" Mr. Farley stopped what he was doing when she showed up there a little past 9:30. "I didn't think I had you scheduled 'til noon today."

"You didn't, but Anne Marie told me you were kind of busy, so I thought I'd come in and help out if that's okay."

Melody saw Zach pop out of the back room where he'd been working, and she didn't miss the pleased expression on his face when he saw her.

"Okay? It's more than okay. If you don't mind working out front, I can work with Zach and get this done a lot quicker. Fantastic! Thanks a lot, Mel." Mr. Farley chuckled. "I guess we'll have to make you some kind of 'Employee of the Month' button or something."

The morning flew by, as did the afternoon, and Melody was shocked when Zach came up behind her and asked if she was going to work the night shift too.

"Oh my gosh, I had no idea it was after 4:00. No wonder my stomach has been growling at me."

"Well, I'm outta here now too, so how about grabbing something to eat?"

Before she could answer, Mr. Farley who was getting ready to close for the day said, "Zach, your mom texted dinner's almost ready."

"Yeah, you'd better go ahead home." Melody was disappointed, but what else could she say?

"Why don't you join us, Mel? My wife always makes way more than we can handle."

Melody was going to politely decline until she saw the hopeful expression on Zach's face. "Are you sure she won't mind?" Melody had met Mrs. Farley several times when she came to help at the bookstore, and she seemed to be an easy-going type, but an extra person for dinner at the very last minute might be pushing it.

"She'll love it. Trust me!" Zach grabbed her hand and whisked her out the door before she could change her mind. "And I think you'll like my mom's cooking. I don't know what we're having, but it'll be good."

"Wait, gimme a minute." Melody pulled her phone out of her back pocket and shot her mother a quick text explaining that the

Farleys had invited her for dinner and asking if she minded. She let out her breath when, after several seconds, she got the okay.

Then it hit her. She was going to meet her boyfriend's parents! Well, no, not really. She had already met them. She worked for them after all... but this was different. Melody had never been to Zach's house. She knew which one it was, but to be invited there... *Wow!*

Since she'd spent time with every member of the family—at least that's what she thought—she was surprised by the butterflies fluttering about in her stomach.

However, Melody discovered there were two members of the family Zach had never mentioned. One had four legs and, smelling the scent of Star, was all over her the moment she entered the house. She learned the dog's name was Sophie and that she was an extremely friendly Golden Retriever, especially when getting her belly scratched.

Busily keeping Sophie entertained, Melody didn't see the eldest member of the family until she heard her say, "Ah, so is this your new girlfriend, Zachary?"

Melody looked up to see a woman, probably in her mid-fifties or early sixties, smiling sweetly, unaware of the effect the words *new girlfriend* would have.

"Yes, Grammy. I'd like you to meet my girlfriend, Melody Patterson."

He had finally said it. *My girlfriend.* She forgot all about the grandmother's word *new* in there... at least for now.

14 A New Status

The summer of 2017 was a memorable one for Melody for many reasons, the most important of which was officially becoming Zach Farley's girl. At first she hesitated to tell her best friend about her new relationship status, but within twenty-four hours it had come blurting out.

"Dee, you're not gonna believe this... he actually introduced me to his Grammy as his *girlfriend!*"

"No way! Really? And his parents were there? What did they say?"

"I don't know, but I remember they were all smiling, and I know my face got red. I could feel it." The conversation had gone on for some time with lots of giggling in between comments, when Melody got around to asking what had been on her mind. "So anyway... do you mind? I mean will it bother you?"

"Well, of course." Denise's tone was full of indignation before she burst out laughing. "You really are dense! You're my best friend, fool. Don't you think I'm happy for you? Besides, I've already got my eye on Ben." Denise hopped off the bed and strutted over toward the mirror, fluffing her hair. "He's not going out with Jasmine anymore, yanno."

"Oh well, in that case, *dahling*, I'm sure he's all yours."

More fits of laughter brought Chelsea to the door. "What's so funny?" she asked, arms akimbo. Seeing they were incapable of answering, she rolled her eyes and left them to their merriment.

Eventually the conversation turned to a more serious subject. Melody asked Denise how things were at home and if she'd seen or heard from her dad since he left.

"He wrote each of us—me and Mom—a letter. I'm not sure what hers said, but I know it made her cry. Mine said how sorry he was, and he swears he's going to turn his life around." Denise sat cross-legged on the bed and stared out the window for what seemed the longest time before going on.

When she turned her gaze back, Melody saw the sadness and something else she didn't understand in her now glassy eyes. "Mom says she'll believe it when she sees it, but you know what? I think he really means it this time."

"Of course he does." Melody wanted to make her friend feel better even if she wasn't so sure it was true. "Maybe this is what he needed, huh? At least we can hope it's true."

Denise said the most important part of the letter was his acknowledgment that he was an alcoholic. "He said he went to his first meeting already... and he's going to go to one every day. Do you think he will? I mean he never admitted he had a problem before, so..."

Melody wasn't sure what to think, but she wanted it to be true for Denise's sake. "My dad used to say, 'If something is really important to you, if you want it *really* badly, then tell God. Pray about it. You know God answers prayer.' So maybe do that... and I will too."

She decided to leave it at that. Hearing how we may not always get the answer we're looking for but God knows best probably wasn't what Denise needed to hear right now.

It would be a while before anyone would know God's answer, but it was an answer worth waiting for. In the meantime, Denise and her mother were at peace and without day-to-day fear of what he might say or do.

***

Melody and Zach spent a lot of time together all through the summer months, and true to her word, Denise got a boyfriend of her own. Before long she and Ben and Melody and Zach were seen together everywhere.

Chelsea and Bobby had grown more serious despite Chelsea's desire to avoid entanglements before going abroad. Bobby Longo was in love, and he was persistent. It was in August, the Saturday before her departure, that Chelsea was asked the big question, and she was shocked... but not as shocked as their mother.

15 It's all too much

"I wasn't expecting it, Mom, and I almost didn't accept, but... well, next thing I know I was saying yes."

Judy stared at the little diamond on Chelsea's finger, then slowly lifted her gaze to her older daughter's expectant face. "But Chels, you're only eighteen. And you're leaving for Paris Tuesday. This is crazy!" She leaned back against the kitchen counter and tried to catch her breath. She saw the crestfallen look on Chelsea's face and regretted hurting her, but what did she expect? "I'm sorry, sweetie. I mean it. I want to be happy for you... and I am. I mean I'm happy you have someone special, but I just think it's all happening too fast."

Judy looked at her youngest daughter trying to read her reaction, but Melody gave no clue how she felt about this whole ridiculous situation.

"Listen, Mom. You need to take a breath. It's not like we're planning to run down to the church and get married today. I told Bobby I would agree to marry him but only if he was willing to wait until I finish culinary school and he finishes at the Police Academy."

Judy was relieved to hear that at least. "You'll both still be so young though. What do you think, Melody?"

"What difference does that make?" Melody grabbed her phone off the island, slid off the barstool, and left the room with Star right behind her.

"Mom, listen." Chelsea put her hands on her mother's shoulders. "I may not want a big fancy wedding, but I do want a church wedding with the white dress and flowers and a nice reception afterwards... and all that takes time and planning... so, let's just breathe, okay?"

Since when did my daughter become the mother? "All right. I'm breathing." Looking into her daughter's eyes, Judy realized what she had to do. What she had to say. "All right, come here." She pulled her daughter into a tight embrace, trying not to smother her. "You know I love you, and I just want you to be sure. I want you to be happy... to have your happily ever after."

"I am, Mom. I really am. I want what you and Dad had."

Judy held Chelsea at arm's length, and she could see it was true. "Then I'm happy for you."

But not everybody was happy.

16 Too Many Changes

Melody left the kitchen. She couldn't stand listening to the whole engagement conversation, and when her mother asked how she felt about it—what could she say after all—but she didn't go far. Standing in the next room, she heard the rest of the conversation.

Happily ever after... ha! There's no such thing.

Melody knew better. Just when you think everything is wonderful, something will come along and ruin things for sure. Things like death... and people leaving.

She wanted to stay mad at Chelsea for accepting her boyfriend's proposal. She didn't want to talk to her at all, but soon Chelsea would be gone—an ocean away—so she grudgingly acquiesced.

They spent the entire day together Monday until Bobby came and whisked her sister away for the evening. Even then, Melody waited up until her sister got home after midnight and kept her awake for another hour talking before they both fell asleep in Chelsea's bed at nearly two in the morning.

The three Patterson women said their tearful goodbyes at the airport the next day before Chelsea went through security. The ride home was a solemn one. Melody felt like she'd lost her best friend, but remembered that at least she had Denise. With that thought came the realization that her mother didn't have a best friend.

Melody's parents were friends with several other couples, but after Ken died, Judy rarely saw them. She had lots of acquaintances and friends at work, but no one she was close to. So, it was the daughter who felt the need to take care of the mother now. She was sure her mom would be lost without Chelsea.

Melody struggled to think how she could help. "Mom, do you want to have a race when we get home?"

"Oh, I'd love to, Mel, but we'll have to make it a quick one. Sterling and I thought the three of us could run in to the harbor for crab legs tonight. He said he'd pick us up around 4:30 to beat the crowd."

So much for *poor Mom.* "Oh, wow, I'm sorry. I didn't know, and I already made other plans." It was a lie, but Melody thought it was worth the little fib to avoid spending the evening with Sterling Blair. She had learned to accept her mother seeing him, but she didn't have to like it.

17 Running Away

This would be the third Christmas without Ken Patterson, and this year Chelsea wouldn't be home for the holiday either. Now that she was studying art in Paris, she said she couldn't afford to fly home. Melody believed her sister's true reason for staying away had nothing to do with money since Mom had even offered to pay her fare and she still declined.

The real reason was the new man in the leather chair. Every time Melody saw him sitting there, she wanted to scream, *"That's my father's place. Get out!"*

But of course, he wouldn't be going anywhere. When Judy first starting seeing Sterling, both her daughters were shocked, but Chelsea had conceded their mother had a right to be happy and that she was too young to be doomed to living the rest of her life alone.

"But Dad just died," Melody had once said, tears welling up in her eyes with the memory.

"No, Melody. It's been more than two years now and you know it."

Melody was quite aware as she had stumbled through the day on the second anniversary of Ken Patterson's death, and although her mother put on a brave face, Melody had heard her crying in the bathroom. The memory was still fresh in her mind. *How can Mom go out with another man?*

But Judy did go out with another man. First it had been with the group at Parents Without Partners, but before long, the two of them had been going out to dinner alone. *Dating!* Lately Mr. Blair was often having dinner at their house, and her mother was cooking for him. Melody hated it every time she saw him sitting in *Dad's place* at the table. It all just felt so wrong.

Tonight's dinner was one of Melody's favorites, but she had lost her appetite even for her mother's "Pork Chops Supreme." She pushed the food around on her plate trying to come up with an excuse to leave the table and escape this inappropriate scene.

"Have you thought about spending Christmas Eve with us, Sterling?" Judy asked. "You know we'd love to have you... and your daughter, Carol, too."

Melody dropped her fork on her plate. No longer feeling the need for an excuse, she pushed back her chair and stormed out of the room.

"No, don't worry about it," she heard her mother say to Sterling. "She'll be okay. She'll come around."

Come around? I don't think so!

With tears streaming down her face, Melody pulled the duffle out of her closet and stuffed it with clothes, all the money she had saved to buy Christmas presents, and the Bible her parents presented to her as a Confirmation Day gift. She buried her head in Star's collar and wept.

"I'm sorry, girl. I've gotta go." Melody had no idea where she was going. She only knew she couldn't stay here. She couldn't watch Sterling Blair try to take her father's place in this house or in her life. Never!

Judy and Sterling were still chatting in the dining room and didn't hear Melody get her coat and quietly slip out the back door, leaving her furry best friend behind.

She pulled her coat tight against the cold December night air. Reaching into the pockets she found her warm gloves but she wished she had grabbed a hat or scarf when the wind whipped through her hair. The lights at each house on her street allowed her to see where she was going, and everything was familiar, but once out of her own neighborhood, the darkness thickened and her resolve weakened. *What am I doing? Where am I going?*

Leaning against a tree trunk to get her bearings, Melody watched her frosty breath and shivered uncontrollably. *I've got to find someplace to stay.* Pulling her phone out, she called Denise, and filled her in on what was happening. "So, can I stay with you tonight?"

"Gosh, Mel, you know I'd say yes for sure, but don't you remember? We're away for the holidays. We just left for Grammy and Pap's in Myrtle Beach this morning."

Melody had indeed forgotten. Now that Denise's father had been clean and sober for six months, he had moved back in with them, and they were headed to his parents' place for the holidays where he hoped to make amends.

Melody was happy for her friend, but a bad situation had instantly gotten worse for her. "What am I going to do?" She felt her determination wavering.

"Have you talked to Zach about this?"

"No, Dee. It all happened so fast, and besides he and his family already headed for Maryland to spend the holidays with his great aunt, so what could he do?"

"Maybe you'd better go back home, Mel."

"No! I can't. I just can't. I'll figure something out. If only Chelsea was here. She'd know what to do."

"Yeah, she'd make you go back home." When Melody didn't respond, Denise hesitated before saying, "All right, if you won't go home, I have an idea."

"Really? What is it?"

"We have a hidden key. You know, like for when one of us locks ourselves out. I guess you could let yourself in and stay in my room for tonight."

"For real? Are you sure?"

"Yeah, but be quiet and don't light the place up. The cops would come for sure if they think someone's in the house. I'll text you the code for the garage, and the key is under the first paint can on the shelves by the kitchen door."

Melody thanked her a million times, ended the call and headed for Denise's house six blocks away. Each set of passing headlights set her heart racing faster. When she finally got inside her friend's garage, and the door closed behind her, she heaved a sigh of relief. She found the key right where Denise said it would be, and with trembling fingers, unlocked the entry to the mud room, stepped in, and rested against the door, relieved to be out of the frigid evening air.

Grateful for the few lights the family left on as a signal someone might be home, and grateful she'd spent so much time at Denise's that the house was almost as familiar as her own, Melody quickly made her way to her friend's bedroom, dropped her duffle on the floor, collapsed on the bed, and waited for her heart to stop pounding.

Then her phone vibrated. A quick check showed her mother was trying to reach her. *Oh crap. She already knows I left.* Melody considered answering, but on second thought she changed her mind and let it go to voicemail. The sound of her mother's frantic voice implored her to respond in some way, but she wasn't ready to talk to her. *What would I even say?* Instead, she shot off a quick text—Don't worry. I M OK—then turned her phone off.

Exhausted from her own worries, within minutes Melody fell asleep. When she awoke hours later, she was disoriented and had to shake off the cobwebs before remembering where she was and what had brought her there. It was 4:00 A.M. Too dark to read, and Denise had warned her that a light coming on in a bedroom of a vacant house in the middle of the night was not a good idea. But unable to get back to sleep, Melody took her phone and her Bible into the bathroom and closed the door.

A quick check of her messages flooded her with guilt. Judy Patterson had responded to her text with more desperate questions. "Where are you? Why won't you answer your phone? Why did you leave?" and pleas of "Please call. Please come home. We'll work it out." The last two texts stunned her. "Melody, I asked Sterling to leave. I won't have him here for Christmas. I didn't mean to hurt you." And "Call me. PLEASE!"

There were also two missed calls from Chelsea. Melody was desperate to hear her sister's voice, but when she played the message, she was crushed.

"Mel, what are you doing? Are you okay? Mom is frantic. What the heck? Call me. I don't care what time. Just call me."

With the time difference, Melody figured it was about ten in the morning in Paris, so she placed the call and held her breath.

She was relieved to hear Chelsea's voice even though her words piled on more guilt. "What were you thinking, girl? And where the heck are you?"

"I'm at Denise's... they're away, but she said I could stay here tonight. But you can't tell Mom... please!"

"All right, I won't, but then you have to call her yourself. And you *must* go home."

"But Chelsea, you don't know what it was like seeing Mr. Blair sitting there in Dad's place at the table... and then when Mom invited him to spend Christmas Eve with us... I, I just couldn't take it." The thought of it made her throat tighten as she tried to choke back a new flood of tears.

"I get it, Mel... but this isn't the answer. I'm sorry I'm not there with you, but you know Mom loves you, and not knowing where you are is tearing her up."

"I don't want to hurt her, but..."

After saying goodbye to her sister, Melody put down the phone and picked up the Bible. She opened to a random page and found herself staring at the commandments. They were all printed the same on the page, yet one seemed to be larger and in bold print. It jumped out at her.

Honor thy father and thy mother.

She closed the book, turned off the light, and went back to the bedroom. Sitting on the side of the bed in the dark room, Melody could still see the words... Honor thy father and thy mother.

How can I honor my father if I let this intruder take his place?

Yet the words kept repeating in her head until she wanted to scream. The vibration of her phone on the nightstand where she'd laid it interrupted her thoughts. It was a text from Chelsea.

"Hi, Mel. I thought of something that might help you. What would Dad want you to do?"

Melody flopped back against the pillow and sobbed. She knew what she had to do.

As soon as it was light outside, she bundled up, and fifteen minutes later found herself standing in front of her mother. After a mere heartbeat of a pause, they were in each other's arms and both in tears—Judy's were tears of relief and Melody's of regret.

The days before Christmas Eve flew by quickly after that tearful reunion, and it was amazing how much had changed in that short time. Once Melody opened her heart to Sterling, she discovered he wasn't such a bad guy after all, and he reassured her he wasn't trying to take her father's place in her life but that he cared for her mother and hoped Melody could find a place for him in her heart.

By then Melody knew Sterling was important to her mother's happiness, and it was genuinely good to see her mother smiling more. Melody resolved to find room in her heart for Mr. Blair for her mom's sake. She even told him she hoped he and his daughter would join them for Christmas Eve.

So it was that Melody, Judy, Sterling, and Carol were putting on their coats to head out to the Christmas Eve service when they heard the front door open.

"Surprise! Merry Christmas!"

No sooner were the words hanging in the air, than Chelsea was nearly smothered in hugs. Her decision to come home for Christmas after all was the best present Melody could have received, and when she sang the Hallelujah Chorus at church that evening, she felt the joy that had been missing for the last two years. As the final chord was played, she looked heavenward. *We're going to be all right, Dad.*

Back at the house, everyone gathered around with their cup of warm cider, and, as her mother had suggested, Melody sat in the big leather chair with Star curled up at her feet.

She picked up the Bible—the one her father had always read from—opened it to the Christmas story in the book of Luke, and began reading. "And it came to pass in those days, that there went out a decree from Caesar Augustus, that all the world should be taxed." The final words swam before her eyes, but she didn't need to see the printed page. She spoke the words she had so often heard her father read. "And the shepherds returned, glorifying and praising God for all the things that they had heard and seen, as it was told unto them."

Acknowledgments

I would like to thank Kathie Shoop for first suggesting the idea of writing a Christmas story, Demi Stevens for helping me see it through, and all those at the Mindful Writers Retreat for providing an inspirational setting.

About the Author

Gloria Bostic is a retired special education teacher from York, Pennsylvania. As a Masters level clinical psychologist, she also worked with women and children to help them overcome abuse. She lives in Dover, PA, with her husband, Lee, and enjoys spending time with her three sons and all her grandchildren.

Also by Gloria Bostic…

Deception Bridge (Book 1)

Valerie Reed is plagued by migraines, insomnia, and a growing anxiety that her happily-ever-after is about to come crumbling down. Tormented by the fear of losing her husband of nearly thirty years, she hangs onto the one thing she knows she can count on – her friendship with the women in her bridge group. They provide a safe-haven with warmth, laughter, and trust… until that trust is broken.

As Val searches for a way to save her marriage and learn to trust again, her life and her bridge group go through unanticipated transformations. Their lives will never be the same, and Val wonders if the power of prayer will be enough to save them all.

Broken Contracts (Book 2)

Through faith and forgiveness Valerie and Andy Reed's marriage has survived and grown stronger in spite of Andy's brief affair five years ago. However, the consequences of his tryst with Susan Walters, a former member of Val's bridge group, may now turn their world upside-down once again.

As Susan's marriage falls apart, all she wants is to be a good mother to the child she had always longed for… yet her life is becoming unmanageable as she continually succumbs to the need for her next drink.

When Valerie, Bonnie, Sarah, and Kathy gather around the bridge table, they share more than the game. Only time will tell what's in the cards.

Premonition Bridge (Book 3)

A threat… A former client warns that her husband is wildly angry that she left him and blames her therapist, Sarah Reed, for ruining his life. He vows to get even.

A disappearance… A member of the Reed family mysteriously disappears without a trace. The only clues to the victim's whereabouts may come from mystifying messages in drawings and dreams.

A reuniting... Family members separated, relationships lost, friendships dissolved... Will prayer and forgiveness be enough for the bridge club ladies to find resolution from the chaos that has invaded their lives?

Out of the Storm

Greta Friedman travels from victim to victory in this story of a young woman's search for the life she's been denied. A childhood filled with loss and abuse leaves her desperate to find love and normalcy, but as a young adult Greta is frustrated by unanswered prayers and a pattern of relationships that end badly... until she meets someone special. When Gabe Engel mysteriously comes into her life, Greta begins the journey that will give her the strength to escape impending danger and finally make her dreams a reality.

Watercolor Whispers (Book 1)

Art therapist Mia Reed has a calling to help her patients as well as a special gift... paintings that unlock mysteries and help solve crimes. However, Freddie Alessi—an assault victim whose wife has gone missing—leaves every session more disturbed than when he arrived... almost as disturbed as Mia feels about his charming and attractive older brother Anthony. Her brain says run, but his fervent kisses keep drawing her back.

Detective Ron Bishop is intrigued by Mia's gift as he struggles to solve missing persons and murder cases. But when Mia's hand is guided by an outside force, can the clues in her drawings lead to the killer and answer the questions in time?

Whispered Warnings (Book 2)

Mia Reed's artwork is a gift from a higher power and holds clues that help solve mysteries. Detective Ronald Bishop, the man she loves, is desperate to find his twin sister who disappeared fifteen years ago. But in the meantime he's lured to follow Mia to her hometown, where a clinical psychologist has jumped to her death. Or did she? When two more single women suffer the same fate, everyone realizes these are not suicides. A serial killer has invaded their peaceful small town! Will Mia's gift help them catch a murderer before he strikes too close to home?

Waiting for the Whisper (Book 3)

Mia's faith is shaken when she discovers a long-held family secret about her family's rock—her beloved grandfather. When she longs to lean on her fiancé, Detective Ron Bishop, for support, his attention is more focused on collecting evidence to prove her client's guilt. Meanwhile he's also hunting down the men who murdered his parents and held his sister Robin captive for years.

Mia understands that putting the kidnappers away is the only thing that will end Robin's nightmare of fear, but she wonders if Ron will ever be there for her again as the clock ticks down to their wedding day. Will Ron's sudden concern for his twin stand in the way of their "happily-ever-after?"

The Greatest Aunt

It's a scary time for Flora when she learns her parents must go away. She will have to go live with her great-aunt, but can't understand why they call her great. Flora happily discovers why and agrees!